Day three of the hamster hunt.

Thursday, we got more clues from other kids at South School.

"I saw him under the piano."

"He was in the girls' bathroom."

"We almost caught him by the food cabinet in the cafeteria."

Friday morning when the class went down to the bathroom, we checked on the Havahart Trap again.

Nothing.

The peanut butter was still in the trap. Untouched.

"Boys and girls, Yi has been missing for three days now. But he's been sighted by so many students, we know he is alive. Let's not give up."

SONG LEE AND
THE HAMSTER HUNT

PUFFIN BOOKS ABOUT ROOM 2B

Horrible Harry and the Ant Invasion
Horrible Harry and the Christmas Surprise
Horrible Harry and the Drop of Doom
Horrible Harry and the Dungeon
Horrible Harry and the Green Slime
Horrible Harry and the Kickball Wedding
Horrible Harry and the Purple People
Horrible Harry in Room 2B
Horrible Harry's Secret
Song Lee and the Hamster Hunt
Song Lee and the Leech Man
Song Lee in Room 2B

SONG LEE AND
THE HAMSTER HUNT

BY SUZY KLINE
Pictures by Frank Remkiewicz

PUFFIN BOOKS

E
K65sLh

PUFFIN BOOKS
Published by the Penguin Group
Penguin Putnam Books for Young Readers,
345 Hudson Street, New York, New York 10014, U.S.A.
Penguin Books Ltd, 27 Wrights Lane, London W8 5TZ, England
Penguin Books Australia Ltd, Ringwood, Victoria, Australia
Penguin Books Canada Ltd, 10 Alcorn Avenue, Toronto, Ontario, Canada M4V 3B2
Penguin Books (N.Z.) Ltd, 182-190 Wairau Road, Auckland 10, New Zealand

Penguin Books Ltd, Registered Offices: Harmondsworth, Middlesex, England

First published in the United States of America by Viking,
a division of Penguin Books USA Inc., 1994
Published by Puffin Books, 1996
Reissued 2000

1 3 5 7 9 10 8 6 4 2

Text copyright © Suzy Kline, 1994
Illustrations copyright © Frank Remkiewicz, 1994
All rights reserved

THE LIBRARY OF CONGRESS HAS CATALOGED THE VIKING EDITION AS FOLLOWS:
Kline, Suzy.
Song Lee and the hamster hunt / by Suzy Kline; pictures by Frank Remkiewicz.
p.   cm.
Summary: When Song Lee's hamster escapes from its cage in Room 2B, the class
members and other students in South School become involved in the search for him.
ISBN 0-670-84773-9
[1. Schools—Fiction. 2. Hamsters—Fiction. 3. Korean Americans—Fiction.]
I. Remkiewicz, Frank, ill. II. Title.
PZ7.K6797Sm 1994 [Fic]—dc20 93-44108 CIP AC

This edition ISBN 0-14-130707-2

Printed in the United States of America

RL: 2.4

Dedicated with ♡ love ♡ to my class:

Seth Begey	Jessica Gunraj
Ross Bowman	Daniel Hickey
Tiffany Cardente	Emily Jamison
Darren Carey	Meghan Lavallee
Charlton Chittem	Mathew Mansfield
Jeffrey Clark	Kristopher McDonnell
Bobby Cyrs	Nicole Pelchat
Danielle DiMeo	Eric Pleil
Scott Donaghy	Jonathan Pond
Kristen Dubreuil	Timea Sarkozi
Joshua Dy	Robin Schrager
Billie Jean Fendley	Ryan Snyder
Rosanne Field	Tonya Sweeney
Eric Ford	Jared Tkacs
Michael Fusco	Thomas Woznicki
Danielle Gagnon	Michele Zordan

♡ And my aide, Carol van Czak

♡ And our custodian, Ed Beausoleil

♡ And **Fluffy,** our class hamster in the spring of 1993, who escaped from his cage and was found by Mr. Beausoleil in the school a week later.

Contents

Habits and Hamsters   1

Yi Escapes!   14

Sidney to the Rescue   29

King Fuzzball   42

Habits and Hamsters

Tuesday morning we all gathered around the science table to watch Song Lee's hamster. He has been in Room 2B for two weeks. I like his name. It's Yi and rhymes with Song Lee.

Tikka tikka tikka tikka.

"Hear him drink from water bottle?" Song Lee said. Then she looked at me.

1

"Doug, do you think it sounds like typewriter?"

I listened.

Tikka tikka tikka tikka.

"It sure does!"

We laughed.

Then Harry came over. "Can I hold Yi?"

Song Lee got up and asked the teacher. Miss Mackle nodded and joined us at the science table.

Song Lee lifted the side door of the cage and reached across the cedar chips. When she accidentally moved the food dish away from the corner, the hamster shoved it back.

Push. Push. Push.

"Yi likes to eat in the corner," Song Lee said.

"Amazing," Miss Mackle replied. "We are all creatures of habit."

Sidney spit out a hangnail he had been chewing.

"That's gross," Mary snapped. "You shouldn't bite your nails. That's a bad habit."

Sidney glared at Mary. "So? You've got bad habits too."

"Do not."

"Do too," Sidney replied. "You eat too much and you boss people around."

"Well, you're King Tattletale!"

"Miss Mackle," Sidney said. "Mary just called me a tattletale."

"All right, you two. Let's be kind to one another. Look, Song Lee is taking Yi out of the cage."

Harry made a bowl with his hands. When Song Lee placed the hamster inside, Harry started making cooing noises.

"Ahhhhhhh! Oooooooh! You're just

4

like a little fuzzy golden tennis ball."

"He hardly has a tail," I said.

"That's how you can tell the difference between hamsters and gerbils," Mary explained. "By the tail. Gerbils have long tails. Hamsters have tiny tails."

"Can I hold him?" Sidney asked.

"It's still Harry's turn," Miss Mackle said.

"Oooooh, you cute little fuzz ball!"
Harry said. Then he petted Yi gently
with his fingers.

"My turn!" Sidney snapped.

"Shhh! Yi is getting sleepy," Mary
said.

We all watched Harry rock Yi back
and forth, back and forth, as he sang:

"Rock-a-bye Yi-Yi,
Soft in my hand.
You are King Fuzzball,
King of the land.

"When you wake up,
I'll tickle your tail.
We'll go on adventures
And drink ginger ale."

When Harry finished singing, he
flashed a toothy smile.

Yi was asleep.

6

The rest of us smiled, too, except Sidney. He was mad. "Harry is hogging the hamster."

Miss Mackle looked up at the clock. "Uh oh! It's writing time. Better put Yi back in his cage now."

"No fair! I didn't get a turn!"

"I'm sorry, Sidney," Miss Mackle replied. "You can hold Yi first, next time."

Sidney made a long face.

The teacher watched Song Lee put the hamster in the wire cage and hook the lock.

"Song Lee," Miss Mackle asked, "how did you happen to call him Yi?"

"It is name of my cousin in Korea. I name hamster after him."

"I like it." Miss Mackle smiled.

We watched Yi gnaw and sniff at the wire. When he poked his nose and whiskers between the bars, we laughed.

After I returned to my seat, I started writing about Yi in my notebook. Song Lee was drawing a picture of Harry singing to the hamster. Sidney sharpened his pencil; then he stopped by the hamster cage. Miss Mackle was too busy writing in her own notebook to notice.

Fifteen minutes later, Mary got up and looked at the hamster. "Something's wrong with Yi!"

We all ran back to the table.

"He's drenched!" Miss Mackle exclaimed.

Harry held up a fist. "When I find out who did this, I'm sending him to the moon. *Nonstop!*"

"Poor Yi. He's sopping wet!" Miss Mackle said. "Just look at the cedar chips! They're waterlogged. Who would do such a thing?"

Song Lee opened the cage door and picked up the wet hamster. "I get my hankie and dry you off, Yi-Yi."

Everyone looked at the water bottle. It was empty.

"Someone sprayed Yi!" I said. Then I looked at Sidney. "You were over at the cage during writing! Was it you?"

Sidney shrugged. "Everyone squeezes that water bottle."

Miss Mackle lowered her eyebrows.

10

"*We* just squeeze it a teensy bit!" Mary replied. "We don't *hose down the hamster.*"

Sidney chewed a nail and then spit it out. "I thought it would be fun to give Yi a . . . a shower."

"Sidney!" Miss Mackle exclaimed. "You sprayed that entire bottle?"

"He sure did!" Mary snapped. "He has another bad habit—hosing down hamsters!"

Harry got Sidney in a headlock.

"Help! Harry's sending me to the moon!"

"*Nonstop,*" Mary added.

Miss Mackle separated the boys. "Fighting doesn't solve anything. Harry, go back to your seat and put your head down. Sidney, I want you to write a letter of apology to Yi right now."

Sidney wrinkled his face. "Hamsters can read?"

"No," Miss Mackle replied, "but they do have feelings. If we don't take good care of our classroom pets, we won't be able to keep any. Yi needs a clean, *dry* cage. And he does not need a morning shower!"

Sidney got some green lined paper and sat down at the science table.

"I'm sorry. I won't do it again."

I looked over at Song Lee. She was patting Yi's wet fur with her cherry-blossom handkerchief. Harry was taking something out of his lunch box.

"This is for Yi," he said.

We looked at the orange slice in Harry's hand.

"Thank you, Harry," Song Lee said. "Yi likes orange almost as much as peanut butter."

"He does?" Sidney said, laying his letter on the table.

Song Lee nodded.

Then we all read Sidney's letter:

Dear Yi,
   I'm ~~Sur~~ glad Song Lee Brot you to class
   I lick ~~your fat~~ you a lot
   I will nevr giv you a shower agen. Just a bath   HA! HA! HA!
   Just Kiding   I'm Sorry
      Yur pal Sid

← Me and Yi
ture love

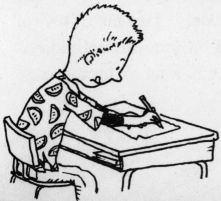

Yi Escapes!

It happened the very next morning when we came to school.

"*He's gone!*" Mary screamed.

"The hamster's cage is empty!" I said. "Someone left the cage door open."

Harry got down and started crawling around the floor. "Yoohoo, Yi! Yo, where are you Yi? Come on out, buddy!"

Song Lee put her hand in the cage

and checked the cedar chips. "Some-times he hide."

Mary pointed her finger at Sidney. "Did you let him out?"

"No! I wouldn't do that. Before I went home yesterday, I reached in his cage and gave him a few pets. I wanted him to know I was sorry. After that, I made sure I closed the door."

"And you hooked it?" I said.

"What hook?"

"*Sidney!*" we all shouted.

Song Lee put her head down. "Yi is not in cage. He is in school . . . some-where. I hope he is safe."

Sidney started crying. "I didn't know he could get out."

Miss Mackle came over and patted Sidney on the back. Then she touched Song Lee's shoulder. "I think we'll find him. Let's look around our room right

now. Especially in the corners and nooks and crannies."

Sidney sat down at the science table and stared at the empty cage. "Yi is probably lying out there in the street somewhere, squished by a car. A golden splat on the road."

"*Sidney, stop!*" Mary yelled. Then

she looked inside the bin of books that was on the floor. "Not here."

Song Lee and I moved the bookcase and looked behind it. Nothing.

Ten minutes later, Miss Mackle said, "We won't give up hope, but we have to carry on. It's writing time."

"I'm calling my story 'The Big Escape,'" Harry said.

"Mine is 'The Mystery of the Golden Juices on the Road,'" Sidney replied.

Mary shot Sidney a look.

Song Lee didn't write anything.

I listed places where Yi might have gone in the school.

Just about everybody wrote about Yi.

After lunch, Miss Mackle wrote a math problem on the board. When everyone started talking, Miss Mackle turned around. "I would like everyone's attention please."

Harry ignored the teacher and talked to me.

"Do you think Yi is hiding in the teachers' room, Doug? There's always food in there."

Miss Mackle wrote Harry's name on the board. "Now, who else isn't paying attention?"

Sidney looked over at Song Lee. Her Magic Markers were making a squeaking noise. And they smelled. "How come *she* gets to draw and we don't?" Sidney tattled.

Miss Mackle walked over to Song Lee's desk. "You're drawing during math time?"

"Uh oh," Mary whispered. "What if Song Lee gets her name on the board?"

"Look," Ida whispered back. "Song Lee turned her picture over so no one can see."

"What are you drawing, Song Lee?"
Miss Mackle asked.

One tear rolled down Song Lee's cheek. Slowly, she held up her picture. It was a poster that said:

HELP!
Our Hamster Escape
Bring to Room 2B If Seen
Watch Where You Step!

Under the words was a picture of two big sneakers. One was about to step on a hamster.

When Miss Mackle closed her math book, it made a loud noise:

BLAM!

Mary and Ida jumped.

"What a brilliant idea!" the teacher exclaimed. "A poster campaign! If we plaster the school walls with posters, *all* the students at South School can help us look for Yi."

Song Lee wiped her eyes and smiled. "I share my new Magic Markers."

"Mary," the teacher said. "Pass out art paper to everyone."

"Yes, Miss Mackle!"

"*Yahoo!*" Sidney shouted.

Harry rubbed his hands together. "I have a great idea for my poster."

We got busy drawing as soon as we got paper.

Miss Mackle made one suggestion for

Song Lee's poster. "Just add a *d* to *escape*."

Song Lee nodded. "Father remind me to add *s* and *ed* on my words. Reminds! I try harder."

Miss Mackle squatted down next to Song Lee's desk so they were eye to eye. "You have only been in America for one year and you have learned *so* much English. You speak beautifully, Song Lee."

Song Lee covered her face with her hands. She does that sometimes when she gets embarrassed.

Thirty minutes later the class had finished. Some of us even made two posters. I kind of liked mine. It was one big shoe about to step on a hamster— kind of like Song Lee's—but then I drew a big black line across the picture. Like the *No Smoking* sign.

Harry made a huge pencil drawing. It was a hamster that was crying:

Save me from the monsters in South School!

I'm Lost! Return me to Room 2B.

In the background were bats, Count Dracula, the Frankenstein monster, and a picture of Sidney.

Miss Mackle said he had to erase Sidney's name.

Sidney drew a car running over a hamster. His poster said:

Find Yi before it's too late!

Return him to Room 2B.

Miss Mackle let us go in pairs and put up our posters around the school. We plastered them everywhere. Except over the fire-alarm box. Mr. John, our custodian, said to leave that space open.

Just before we went home that day, a fifth grader appeared at our door. "I

saw a hamster in the boys' bathroom. I tried to get him, but he ran away."

We all cheered!

"He's alive and well!" Miss Mackle said. "I'll buy a Havahart Trap and we'll put it in the boys' bathroom tomorrow."

Thanks to Song Lee, our hamster hunt had some new clues! I'm sure glad she wasn't paying attention in math.

Sidney to the Rescue

Thursday, we got more clues from other kids at South School.

"I saw him under the piano."

"He was in the girls' bathroom."

"We almost caught him by the food cabinet in the cafeteria."

Friday morning when the class went down to the bathroom, we checked on the Havahart Trap again.

Nothing.

The peanut butter was still in the trap. Untouched.

"Boys and girls, Yi has been missing for three days now. But he's been sighted by so many students, we know he is alive. Let's not give up."

"I hope he doesn't starve to death," Sidney said.

We all nodded.

When we got back to class, Miss Mackle tried to cheer us up. "We don't want Yi to return to a messy room. Let's clean it for him!" When she saw my name tag all curled up and torn, she added, "Let's make new name tags for our desks, too."

"Can I make one for Yi?" Song Lee asked.

"Good idea!" the teacher replied. Then she smiled. "But I want everyone else to print his or her *full* name."

Ten minutes later we were all coloring and printing on long strips of art paper.

I held mine up—Doug Hurtuk. I liked the teepees in the corner.

Harry was making ants and spiders all over his name—Harry Spooger.

Mary was making a happy face with braids next to hers—Mary Berg.

Ida was drawing pink ballet slippers all around her name—Ida Burrell.

Suddenly, Sidney tore his up.

Rrrrrrrrrrip!

Miss Mackle came over to his desk. "Is there something wrong, Sidney?"

When he shook his head, the teacher lowered her voice.

"Sidney, you have a new last name now. Your stepfather adopted you. That's special."

Sidney scowled, then he put his head

down on his desk. He wasn't talking to
the teacher.

Miss Mackle took a deep breath,
handed him a new paper strip, and then
walked over to another student.

I was curious. "What is your new last
name, Sid?"

"None of your beeswax."

Harry looked up. "I bet it's Sid the
Squid!"

Sidney gritted his teeth. "I'm glad it's not Harry the Canary!"

Twenty minutes later, Miss Mackle started taping our new name tags on our desks.

When I looked over at Sidney, he was printing his old last name, Taylor.

Miss Mackle didn't say anything. She just reached for a book and read to us the rest of the morning. It was a story about a boy who had a really nice stepfather.

As soon as we got down to the cafeteria for lunch, Harry tried to find out Sidney's new last name. "Anyone know?" he asked.

Song Lee nodded. Then she reached into her brown bag and took out two rice cakes and some fruit. "But I think Sidney should tell. Not me."

"I know too," Mary said. "Sidney invited us all to his mother's wedding in February, remember?"

"That's right!" I said. "Only Harry and I couldn't go. Harry ate a whole box of Valentine chocolates and got sick that weekend. I had to go to my grandmother's."

Ida sipped some milk. "Can I tell them?"

"*No!* My stepfather's last name sounds stupid."

Now Harry and I were *really* curious!

Song Lee put her rice cake down. "It is not stupid, Sidney. It is name of famous skunk. You are honored."

Sidney raised his eyebrows. "I am?"

"He is?" Mary asked. "I didn't know La Fleur was a famous skunk."

"*You told!*" Sidney shouted.

"La Fleur?" Harry and I asked.

"*La Fleur*," Song Lee explained, "means flower in French. Flower is famous skunk in *Bambi*."

"I thought *La Fleur* meant the floor," Sidney replied.

Song Lee giggled. "No! *La Fleur* rhyme with *purr*. Like a cat. It is beautiful name."

"How come you know French?" Mary asked.

"My father know Korean, Chinese, English, and French. He tell me what *La Fleur* means when I come home from wedding."

Harry cracked up. "Sidney *La Fleur!*"

Mary glared at Harry. "You shouldn't make fun of people's last names."

"I'm not. I like Sid's last name. It's his first name that stinks."

Just when Sidney and Harry put up

their fists, Mrs. Funderburke came over to our table. "How's the lasagna, girls and boys?"

"Gooooooood," Harry, Mary, and I said with a big smile.

After she left, Mary brought up the subject again. "I think Sidney La Fleur sounds like . . . like . . . a great French chef."

"Really?" Sidney asked.

"I remember," I said, "when you showed us that picture of you and your stepfather barbecuing on the porch. Those chef hats were neat."

Sidney nibbled on his peanut-butter cookie. "They were? Hmmmmm, my stepfather and I *did* make these."

We all drooled when he showed us the bag of golden-brown cookies.

"Mmmmmmmmmm," we said.

Then Sidney asked permission to go

to the bathroom and left. I noticed he took his bag of cookies with him. He probably thought we'd eat them while he was gone.

Later that afternoon, we checked on the Havahart Trap again.

Nothing.

When we got back to the room, Mary

pointed at the window. "Look at those big black clouds in the sky! I bet there's going to be thunder and lightning!"

Song Lee put her head down on her desk. "Yi will be in school all alone."

"All weekend," I groaned.

"Without food," Ida moaned.

Sidney took out a black crayon. "No he won't. I put my four peanut-butter cookies in different corners of the boys' bathroom."

We all looked at Sidney. He was crossing out *Taylor* and writing his new last name.

No one said anything when he misspelled it, and wrote *La Floor*.

Song Lee clapped her hands. "Yi likes peanuts."

Sidney tipped back in his chair like he was some great French chef. "I know. My stepfather and I put one whole cup of peanuts in the cookie recipe. We probably saved that hamster's life."

All of us just crossed our fingers and hoped what Sidney said was true.

King Fuzzball

2B

Monday morning, we all raced over to the hamster cage.

But the door was still open.

"He's not here!" Mary groaned.

"The teacher didn't find him," Ida added.

"*No one* found him," I said.

"And he didn't find his way back," Song Lee said, shaking her head.

Suddenly Sidney came running into

the room. *"He ate one of the cookies! There are just crumbs left!"*

Miss Mackle and Mr. John were talking in the doorway. After the bell rang, the teacher told us she had some wonderful news. We all watched Mr. John walk over to the hamster cage and put something inside.

"Yi?" we all asked.

"Yi-Yi!" Song Lee sighed.

There he was, all curled up in a wet ball of fur. Sleeping in the corner by his food dish.

"It's Yi!" we shouted.

"My Yi-Yi!" Song Lee said.

Harry and I jumped up and down, then we hugged each other. Song Lee hugged Mary and Ida. Harry and Sidney even hugged!

Then we all looked back in the cage. "He looks dead," Sidney said.

"He is very still when he sleeps," Song Lee replied. "If you watch, you see his stomach quiver when he breathes."

We watched.

It quivered.

Sidney groaned. "He's not fluffy anymore. He looks like a tennis ball that bounced into an oil spill."

"He's been through a lot," Mary said.

"I love you, Yi," Song Lee whispered.

"I wish he could talk," I said. "I'd like to know the places he's been."

"Yeah," Harry agreed. "His adventures."

"Who found him?" Mary asked.

Miss Mackle and Mr. John were standing behind us now at the table. "I think, boys and girls, you'll want to hear Mr. John's story."

We all turned and listened to our school custodian.

Slowly he shook his head. "I found him this morning. After that storm we had last weekend, the boiler room was flooded and I was mopping up when I spotted him. Poor thing! He must have been swimming all weekend. He looked exhausted. I put on my gloves and grabbed him under my tool bench."

"Oh, Mr. John," Mary sighed. "You saved Yi! You're our classroom hero!"

When we started clapping, he held up his hand. "No. The credit shouldn't go to me. It should go to *you* and your poster campaign! Everywhere I went in the school, I was reminded to look for that hamster, and not step on him. You had posters all over the place!"

"That was Song Lee's idea," I said. "We should give her a cheer too."

"Good idea, Doug!" Miss Mackle replied.

Song Lee covered her face when we clapped for her.

"What about my peanut-butter cookies?" Sidney added. "They helped too."

We clapped for Sidney.

"*Everyone* helped," Miss Mackle said. "Don't ever forget the power of a poster!

It's called advertising. It helps you get
your message across."

Song Lee looked like she was in deep
thought. We watched her whisper a
message in the teacher's ear.

"Yes!" Miss Mackle said. Then she
looked at Mr. John. "Can you ask Mrs.
Foxworth to make an announcement
for us over the school intercom?"

"Be glad to. But after that, I want those posters off the wall!"

Miss Mackle nodded. Then she whispered something to the custodian.

"What announcement?" Mary asked.

"You'll see," Miss Mackle said. "Please sit down."

We all took our seats and looked up at the intercom. I thought the small holes in the round silver plate looked like the top of a salt shaker.

For three long minutes, Room 2B was pin quiet.

Suddenly, the school secretary cleared her voice over the intercom. *"Uh huh* . . . I have good news for South School this morning. Mr. John found Song Lee's famous hamster, Yi, in the boiler room. After being lost for nearly a week, he is now alive and well in Room 2B!"

We could hear the roar and applause from the other rooms down the hall. We were so happy we started cheering and clapping all over again.

Song Lee went back to the hamster cage and pressed her nose against the

wire. I was probably the only one who heard her softly sing Harry's song:

"Rock-a-bye Yi-Yi,
Soft in my hand.
You are King Fuzzball,
King of the land.

When you wake up,
I'll tickle your tail.
We'll go on adventures
And drink ginger ale."